Jane Lawes

Gym Stars

Friendships and Backflips

USBORNE

Dear Reader,

When I was growing up, I used to live, breathe and dream gymnastics – like Tara, I loved working and working on new moves with my coach as I wanted them to look absolutely perfect!

Gymnastics is a fantastic sport, and with hard work and determination, can be extremely rewarding. It can also be very dangerous however, and without the correct supervision and equipment, can easily lead to injury. Because of this, it's so important to make sure that you practise everything in a gym, where you have the right equipment and supervision.

Since these books have been published, I've loved hearing all your stories about new moves you've tried and competitions you've won, and can't wait to hear more! I just wanted to pass on what my coach used to tell me – always make sure that you practise everything in the safe environment of the gym!

Keep trying, keep working and most importantly, be safe!

Lots of love,

Jane Lawes

www.janelawes.co.uk

Chapter One

Tara Bailey stood at the gate outside Hollypark Secondary School, where she was about to start in Year Seven. She was waiting for her best friends in the world to arrive. She'd been in the same class as Emily and Kate all the way through junior school, but now that was going to change. There were three Year Seven forms at the secondary school, and for the first time since Tara, Emily and Kate were four years old, they were going to be split up.

Students were flooding through the school gates and Tara was worried that she'd get swept along, too. Surrounded by large boys and tall girls, she felt so...*little*. At the top of their junior school, she and her friends had felt like grown-ups compared to the babies sitting in the front row at assembly. Now they had to start all over again. The fact that she was almost lost in her new uniform didn't help. The navy blue V-neck jumper was slightly too big, but the main problem, Tara thought, was the grey skirt, which came down below her knees. Usually she didn't mind being small for her age – it was actually a very good thing in gymnastics, which was all she cared about most of the time – but right now she was wishing that her legs were a little bit longer, or the skirt a little bit shorter. She had gymnastics after school so, as well as her rucksack, she had to carry another bag containing her leotard, a bottle of water and a snack. She felt weighed down already – and she didn't even have any school books to carry yet!

She moved away from the gate a bit so that she wasn't caught in the crowd. Emily should have been on the same bus as Tara, but she'd sent a text to say she'd missed it and was waiting for the next one. Kate's bus came from a different direction. As she waited for them, Tara felt that she'd give anything to be going back to their cosy Year Six classroom this morning. She'd secretly been a little bit jealous when she saw her younger sister, Anna, dressed in the junior school uniform before she left. Lucky Anna still had years ahead of her in the small, friendly playground and the colourful classrooms. Meanwhile Tara would have to find her way to different classrooms for every lesson, and she was sure she'd get lost.

"Tara!" She heard someone squeal her name behind her and turned around.

"Lindsay!" she replied, seeing her friend from Silverdale Gymnastics Club. She had started doing Acrobatic Gymnastics there during the summer and Lindsay was her partner and her best friend at the gym.

For the first time since she'd got out of bed that morning, Tara stopped worrying for a moment. Lindsay ran to give her a hug and Tara felt better instantly. Even though she was in secondary school now, it wasn't as if she didn't know anyone, she reminded herself. A lot of people from her junior school class had moved to the same school as her. And then there were Lindsay and Megan, another Silverdale gymnast, in Year Nine. Even though Tara knew she wouldn't see them much because they weren't in her year, it was nice to know they were there.

"I feel like I haven't seen you for ages!" cried Lindsay, who had been away with her family for the last week of the holidays. "What did I miss at the gym?"

"Nothing much," Tara replied. "We just got back to work on normal things like somersaults and balances." At the end of the summer, Silverdale had performed a big gym display at the town fête. They'd spent weeks working on it, so they hadn't had much time to work on skills like somersaults and backflips. "I practised balances with Sophie, because Megan was on holiday too. We were both abandoned by our partners." Tara grinned cheekily at Lindsay, forgetting for a moment that she was in a strange new school.

"Hey!" laughed Lindsay. "You would have abandoned me too, if your parents had decided to go on holiday to Spain."

"Did you have a good time?" Tara asked.

"It was great – really sunny all week," said Lindsay. "I'm going to ache when I get back in the gym tonight, though!" Tara laughed. Then she saw Emily hurrying towards her, and spotted Kate getting off the bus further down the road. Lindsay looked at her watch. "Better go," she said. "Who's your form tutor?"

"Mrs. James."

Lindsay's face lit up. "She was my Year Seven tutor too!" she exclaimed. "Don't worry, she's really nice. It's so great that we're at the same school now. If you have any problems, come and find me. Have a good day!"

"You too." Tara waved, but her smile faded with worry as Lindsay walked away. *I've still got Kate and Emily,* she reminded herself silently. And as soon as she thought it, they were beside her. They hugged each other quickly and then walked through the gate together.

All of Year Seven had to go to the main hall first to meet their form tutors. They'd had an induction day at the end of last term, so they knew where they were going.

"I wish we were all in the same form," Emily said quietly, just as they reached the door to the hall.

"Me too," said Kate and Tara in unison.

"Let's meet here at break time," said Kate. "It should be easy to find."

"Okay." Tara nodded. Her voice sounded as tiny as she felt. She took a deep breath, and they went inside.

The big room was full of Year Sevens already. Tara and her friends were told where to go by a teacher with three lists. They all smiled nervously at each other, said goodbye, and headed for separate corners of the room. As Tara found her form tutor and had her name ticked off on her list, she couldn't help looking back over her shoulder. Emily was hovering on the edge of her form group and Kate had already been swallowed up by a crowd of blue and grey.

Chapter Two

When everyone in Mrs. James's form had arrived, she took them through a maze of corridors to her classroom. There was some chatter, but Tara, like most of the others, was looking around her, trying desperately to remember the way. She was going to have to learn this route quickly. How long would it take before she stopped getting lost all the time? She couldn't imagine ever knowing her way around this school – it was enormous.

The classroom was painted blue and white, with geography posters stuck to the walls. The tables were set out in rows, with gaps between them and two chairs behind each one. They'd be sitting in pairs, Tara realized. What if there was an odd number? She hoped she didn't get left sitting by herself. Among her new classmates was a group of boys and a few girls from Tara's junior school, but she didn't know any of them very well. At least she was relieved to see that she wasn't the only girl in the class who was small and looked too neatly dressed.

The morning passed quickly; a blur of information and names. The first thing they had to do was chat to someone they didn't know, and then introduce that person to the rest of the class. Mrs. James put them through several rounds of this and then, finally, she gave them their timetables and a map so they could find their classrooms. When they compared their timetables at break, Tara, Emily and Kate discovered that they didn't have many lessons together.

"Does anyone have music after break?" asked Kate. "Or maths for lesson four?" They were walking around the field together, with their timetables in their hands.

Emily frowned, looking at her own timetable. "I have maths then," she said. "But I've got science next, not music."

Tara puzzled over the chart for a moment. "I've got maths lesson four, too!" she said triumphantly.

"Good!" Kate cried dramatically. "It's *so* weird not being in the same class as you two."

"It's horrible," agreed Tara. "But I've got science next, as well," she added, with a relieved smile at Emily.

"Even better," said Emily.

They continued looking at their timetables, and discovered that the only other class all three of them had together was PE. Break was soon over

– another bell rang out across the school – and they reluctantly went back inside.

"I'd better go and find the music room," said Kate, giving them a small wave as she turned away. Tara watched her walking off down the corridor. She was tall enough that her skirt didn't make her look like an unfashionable Year Seven kid, and her dark hair curled around her shoulders. Tara pushed some of her own blonde hair out of her eyes. It had started the morning in a neat ponytail. Her hair, at least, refused to be too tidy.

"Science, then," Emily said cheerfully. "Shall we?"

Tara giggled, glad she didn't have to go and find the science lab all by herself. "We shall!"

"I never thought I'd look forward to maths lessons," sighed Emily that afternoon, when she and Tara met Kate outside the maths classroom. They'd spent lunchtime together but had then gone to their separate forms for registration.

"At least we have *something* all together," said Kate. "Maths can be our time to chat."

But their teacher had other ideas. When they went into the classroom, Mr. Spencer made the whole class stand at the front. Then he told them where to sit. Tara scowled when she realized he was going with alphabetical order. Her surname was Bailey, so she got stuck in the front row, while Emily and Kate (Walter and Wakefield) were given seats together at the back of the room. It was *so* unfair!

The class got through some more getting-to-know-you games, struggled with a few maths questions and wrote down their first piece of homework in their clean, new homework diaries. It was a worksheet of questions to complete by the lesson on Friday. Tara folded the paper inside her new maths exercise book and put it in her bag, thinking that could wait until Thursday evening. Then it was finally time for the last lesson of the day: PE.

When Tara, Kate and Emily walked into the big gym, Tara suddenly started to feel very hopeful about PE lessons. The gym was huge, and she could see loads of gymnastics equipment stacked up at one end. There were big crash mats and a vault, and even a beam pushed against the far wall. She crossed her fingers and hoped they'd get to use it soon.

Miss Isaac, their teacher, kept the lesson fun, and Tara was glad. After the long day, she didn't think she could have managed doing any proper sport. They played Bulldog, Stuck in the Mud and other games until they were worn out. As they trooped off to get changed at the end of the lesson, Emily yawned.

"I'm so tired," she said.

"Me too," agreed Kate. "I'm going to go home and watch TV all evening."

"That sounds exactly like my plan," said Emily, grinning.

"What about you, Tara?" asked Kate.

"My day's not finished yet," said Tara. "I'm going to Silverdale now."

"You're mad," said Kate and Emily at the same time. Tara laughed. Then she yawned, which made her laugh again. She thought they might be right.

She met Lindsay and Megan at the school gate, and they walked the fifteen minutes to the gym together. Lindsay and Megan did most of the talking – Tara was too tired. She was beginning to think that doing gymnastics as well as school was going to be harder than she'd ever imagined.

Chapter Three

Tara absorbed the familiar sights and sounds of the gym as soon as she got there: the thump-thump-thump of someone running down the tumbling track, the sound of a coach calling instructions to a gymnast on the bars, the slightly stale smell and the bright, brilliant blue of the floor. Silverdale Gym Club felt as much like home as her own bedroom. Even though she was exhausted after her first day in Year Seven, coming here felt like a break from timetables and classrooms and getting lost.

The Acrobatic Gymnastics squad she was in worked in pairs and trios and some of the boys worked in a group of four. They all performed balances, and the really good gymnasts did throws as well, where the taller, stronger gymnast, who was the "base" threw their partner, the "top", into the air to turn somersaults before catching them again. Tara and Lindsay couldn't do anything as amazing as that – not yet – but it was all Tara dreamed of.

"Watch out! You nearly kicked me in the head!"

"Sorry, sorry!" gasped Tara. She scrambled up from the mat to see if her partner was hurt. "Are you okay?"

"Fine," Lindsay replied. "That was a close one."

"Close to balancing or close to knocking you out?" Tara laughed.

"Both!" Lindsay grinned.

Tara was glad to have Lindsay back from her holiday. After the warm-up, their coach, Clare, had got them working on a new balance. It was called "standing front angel" and Lindsay had to hold Tara high above her head. Lindsay was taller than Tara, and even though she didn't look very strong, she was able to hold Tara up in balances she'd never imagined being able to do before starting at Silverdale. They'd been partners for two months now, and there was nothing Tara loved more than their training sessions.

"This time we'll do it," said Tara. She was always disappointed when she couldn't get things right straight away. "Ready?"

She and Lindsay stood facing each other. Tara put her hands on Lindsay's shoulders, and Lindsay gripped Tara's hips. Then Tara bent her knees, pushed off the floor and jumped while Lindsay pushed her arms straight up. As she went up into the air, Tara moved her arms out to the side, making her body into a T shape. She ended up balancing flat on Lindsay's hands, so it looked as if she was flying. She began to count seconds in her head. One…two…th— Too late, she was coming down! She put her hands forward so she didn't land on her head.

"Nearly!" she said, upside down on the crash mat.

"We'll do it on Friday," said Lindsay. It was time to go home. Tara sat up and glanced around the floor area her group were using. The others were finishing up, too. Jasmine and Sam, the best gymnasts in the group, were still practising a balance, but Megan and her partner Sophie looked like they'd given up a while ago. Megan was lying on a crash mat chatting to Jack, one of the boys in the group, and Sophie was watching Jasmine and Sam. On the other floor area, behind the beams and bars, Tara could see an Artistic Gymnastics group working on their routines, and right at the back of the gym someone was flying over the vault.

Friendships and Backflips

Her coach, Clare, was talking to two boys and giving them advice on a difficult balance. Then she looked at the clock and raised her voice to talk to everyone. "Before you go, I've got some news." The gymnasts were silent for once, waiting to hear. "I'm going to enter some of you in the Regional Club competition in November." Excitement buzzed around the group.

"What does that mean?" Tara asked Lindsay.

Sam was sitting behind them and she overheard. "You don't know what a competition is?" she said, laughing loudly.

Tara went red and felt stupid. Sam always seemed to be putting her down. Of course she knew what a competition was! She just wasn't sure about the "Regional" bit, and she'd wanted to find out, but now she wished she hadn't asked.

"This competition is for Levels 1 to 4 only, which are the levels we work at in this group," explained Clare, "and gymnasts from clubs all over this area will compete. The pairs and groups who come first in each level will get to compete at the National competition next year."

Tara drank in her coach's words and hugged her knees into her chest. Would she and Lindsay get a chance to compete? They'd learned loads of skills and balances in the last two months, but she was still the newest gymnast in the group. She tried not to get too excited, but she couldn't stop the thought creeping into her head – a real gymnastics competition! She could tell that Lindsay had tensed up next to her and knew her partner was imagining the same thing.

Clare was still talking. "We've got a while to train for it, so there's no need to panic." She paused and smiled. "You just want to know who's going to be competing, don't you?" There was enthusiastic nodding from everyone. "As most of you know, there are different levels for girls' pairs, and the same for boys, as well as categories for trios and groups. We can only enter one pair or group in each category, which means you won't be competing against each other. But it also means I can't take all of you." Tara bit her lip. She told herself silently that she wouldn't be upset if she and Lindsay weren't chosen. There'd be other competitions. She'd work harder and harder, until she *was* chosen. She was concentrating so much on not getting upset that she didn't hear what Clare was saying, "…and Lindsay in Level 2 Girls' Pairs…" It took a second for Tara to work it out. If Lindsay was competing, that meant… Had Clare really chosen her? She looked at Lindsay, who was smiling quietly at her.

"Us?" Tara squeaked.

"Yep!" Lindsay laughed. "Us!"

Tara stared at her and then at Clare. She was actually going to be in a competition! This was what she'd been dreaming of for ages. She thought back to all those times she'd practised gymnastics by herself in the garden, pretending that she was competing in front of a big audience and judges, going for a gold medal. Now she was really going to do just that. She was finally going to be a *real* gymnast!

"Megan and Sophie will compete in Level 3 Girls' Pairs," Clare continued, "and Jasmine and Sam in Level 4 Girls' Pairs." The coach looked at the four boys sitting on the mat nearest to her. "You're the only boys group we've got and I'm sure you'll do a great job in the Level 3 category. Everyone else, I know you've worked really hard, and there are other competitions coming up so you'll work towards them."

The gymnasts who hadn't been chosen did their best to be pleased for the others, but Tara knew how disappointed they must feel. She toned her excitement down so that she didn't make them feel worse.

"Those of you who have taken part in this competition before will know that it's going to take a lot of hard work. Silverdale gymnasts have a reputation for working at a very high standard, and I don't intend to let that slip. I need one hundred per cent commitment from all of you. That means no taking it easy if you've got a bit of a headache, no missing training because you're in the school play, or you're going to visit Grandma. Until the competition, I need all of you here, and completely dedicated. Understood?"

The gymnasts nodded seriously. Tara took it all in. It was going to be tough, there was no doubt about it, but that only made the competition seem even more important.

"You're going to *love* competing," Megan said to Tara as they wandered back to the changing room.

"How many competitions have you done?" Tara asked.

Megan shrugged. "Quite a few," she replied. "It's so much fun!"

"Don't you get nervous?" Tara tugged her school skirt back on over her beloved black and silver leotard, a birthday present from Mum and

Dad in July, and then pulled her hair out of its messy ponytail.

"Of course!" Megan laughed. "That's part of the excitement."

Everyone was talking about the competition.

"What balances do you think Clare will put in our routine?" Lindsay asked Tara.

"Hopefully we'll get to learn some new ones!" Tara replied.

"We were *so* close to winning at Nationals last year," Megan said to Sophie, as they got changed nearby. "That's got to be our aim for this year."

"Let's get through Regionals first!" Sophie said with a laugh.

"You and Sam will breeze through Regionals," Megan said to Jasmine.

"I don't know…" Jasmine replied modestly. "We're competing in Level 4 this year. That's going to be tough."

While Megan, Sophie and Jasmine continued going over all the competitions they'd done before, Tara couldn't help tuning into Sam's conversation with Mel, one of the gymnasts who wasn't going to Regionals.

"Did you hear that stupid question? She's going to let the club down," said Sam. Tara wasn't trying to overhear, but the changing room was small and suddenly it seemed like everyone was listening in. "I don't know what Clare's thinking, putting *her* in a regional competition! She can't even do front angel properly…"

Mel was looking down at her bag and mumbled an answer that could have meant anything.

Lindsay looked worriedly at Tara.

Sam was the oldest girl in the group and she and Tara had got off to a bad start at the beginning of the summer, after Sam had overheard Clare talking about Tara to one of the other coaches. Tara had only caught a few words at the end of the conversation, so she didn't know exactly what Sam had heard, but whatever it was, it seemed to have made her angry with Tara. All summer, Sam had made no secret of the fact that she thought Clare should have chosen a gymnast with more experience to join their group. And she still didn't seem to think Tara was good enough, even though Tara had given everything she'd got in the club's summer display. Tara wished she could keep out of Sam's way, but now they'd be going to a competition together that would be impossible.

Tara grabbed her bag and coat and headed for the door. Everything in front of her looked like it was underwater, but she gritted her teeth, determined not to cry. Just before the door banged behind her, she heard Sam talking again. "What a baby!"

"Shut *up*, Sam!" Tara heard Megan's fierce reply, and then there was silence. She put her coat on in the lobby. The door opened and closed softly and Lindsay and Megan were beside her.

"Ignore her," said Megan.

Tara nodded. She was always being told to ignore Sam.

"We'll prove her wrong," said Lindsay, putting her arm around her partner.

Tara nodded again, vigorously. "We *really* will." Her hurt feelings and her worry that Sam was right bubbled up into determination. Maybe Sam thought she wasn't any good, but that was going to change, starting with the Regional competition. She pushed Lindsay away slightly and looked at her seriously. "Linds, we're going to win."

Chapter Four

Tara did her best to push Sam's words out of her mind. Instead, she thought about what Mum, Dad and her younger sister Anna would say when she told them she was going to be in a competition. She couldn't wait to share it with them, but decided not to say anything on the way home so she could tell them all together. She sat in the car with Mum, completely silent and staring out of the window.

Friendships and Backflips

"Are you okay?" asked Mum. "You're very quiet."

Suddenly, Tara couldn't wait any longer. "I'm going to be in a competition!" The words burst out before she could stop them.

"That's wonderful, darling!" said Mum. "When is it?"

"Oh!" said Tara. "It's in November. But I wasn't going to tell you until I got home because I wanted to tell everyone together."

"Then I won't ask anything until we're home," said Mum.

"I won't mind telling it again." Tara grinned, and she told Mum everything that Clare had said.

"It sounds like Clare's asking a lot from you," said Mum in a worried voice. "Don't you think it might be a bit too much, especially when you're just starting at a new school? Maybe it would be better to settle in at school first, and do the next competition instead of this one."

"Mum!" cried Tara, horrified. "Who knows

when the next competition will be? This one's *important*! If we win, we'll get to compete in the national one. Anyway, I'm sure I'll be fine. The others have been doing competitions as well as school for years and years."

"Well, if you're sure…" said Mum. "We'll just have to be careful that it doesn't get too much for you."

"Woaaahhh," said Anna, when Tara told her. Her brown eyes were wide and she gazed up at Tara, who was sitting on the arm of the sofa. "You're going to be like those gymnasts we saw on TV. They were getting ready for a competition too."

Tara and Anna had watched a group of Acro gymnasts on a TV show during the summer. It was just before Tara had started at Silverdale, and she'd never seen anything like it before. She'd watched them, amazed, and had longed to be like them, just as she'd spent hours in the garden imagining that she was a world-class gymnast like Beth Tweddle. Back then, she'd never thought she'd soon be taking part in a real gymnastics competition. And now she was. In only two months' time, she and Lindsay would perform a routine together, combining acrobatic balances with gymnastics skills like handsprings and walkovers, as well as dance.

"I'm not as good as them," said Tara. "They do big competitions like the European Championships and even the *World* Championships. This is just a regional competition."

"It's not *just* a regional competition," said Dad firmly. "It's your first ever competition, and we're very proud of you."

Tara smiled. She looked down at Anna again, who was still staring up at her as if she was a film star. Even if Sam didn't think she was any good, there were three people here who believed she was.

"There'll be gymnasts competing from loads of

clubs in this area," Tara explained, at break time the next morning. She was sitting with her best friends under a tree at the far end of the school field. They were wrapped up in coats, but it was a sunny day and the ground was dry. It was only their second day at the new school, so it was a relief for all three of them to sit together and chat, just like they'd always done. "In each category, the gymnasts who come first will get to compete in the Nationals!"

"I bet you'll win," said Emily confidently.

Tara laughed, trying not to show how much she wanted Emily to be right. "Probably not," she said. "I haven't been doing Acro for very long. Everyone else will be much better than me."

"No way," said Kate. "You're brilliant. You must be so excited! You'll be just like those gymnasts you see in the Olympics – with the glittery leotards and medals and everything!"

Tara smiled and her eyes sparkled. She pictured herself standing on a podium with a gold medal shining against her leotard. The summer display at Silverdale had been great fun and she'd really felt like she was part of the club – but she wouldn't completely feel like a proper gymnast until she'd been in a competition.

"Even if we don't win," she said, "it'll still be the most exciting thing I've ever done."

"The most exciting thing any of us has ever done," agreed Emily. "And that includes the time Kate got to be in the audience for *The X Factor!*"

"Hey! That *was* exciting!" cried Kate, and she gave Emily a light shove in the arm. Then she giggled and looked at Tara. "But your competition will be even better, because you'll be one of the stars!"

Tara rolled her eyes, but really she loved the fact that her friends were getting carried away. It was so easy to share her enthusiasm with them. At the gym, Sam had ruined it. Remembering what the older gymnast had said, she fell quiet.

"What are you worrying about?" asked Emily.

That was the other good thing about being with her friends – they knew her so well that they could always tell if something was wrong. She shook her head. "Nothing." But that had never worked. It was impossible to hide things from Emily and Kate. They'd been friends for ever and they knew everything about each other. She sighed. "A girl at gym…Sam…she said I shouldn't be in the competition. That I'm not good enough for Regionals." Tara looked down at the grass and blonde hair fell into her eyes. "She said I'll let the club down," she whispered.

"She said *what*?" gasped Emily.

"Rubbish," said Kate immediately.

"Tara, of course you're good enough!" said Emily. "Your coach wouldn't have picked you otherwise."

"I guess," said Tara.

"Em's right," said Kate. "And I bet your other friends at gym don't agree with Sam."

Tara nodded. But even if it was just Sam, it was

hard not to believe that the older gymnast was right. After all, Tara had only been training for a couple of months – how *could* she be as good as the other gymnasts in her group?

"What did the others say?" Emily asked in a gentle voice.

"They told me to ignore her," Tara mumbled. She raised her head, and felt a spark of the same determination she'd shown Lindsay. "And to prove her wrong."

"Yeah!" yelled Kate, raising her hand for a high five. Tara's hands stayed in her lap. Kate looked at Emily, and Emily grabbed one of Tara's hands, lifting it up to hit Kate's. Tara couldn't help laughing.

The bell rang for the end of break and they scrambled up and walked back towards the school building, getting out their maps and timetables again. A group of girls rushed past them, and one of them knocked into Tara and Emily while they had their heads bent over Tara's map. Some boys pushed through as well, still throwing a football back and forth between them.

"Put that ball away!" shouted a passing teacher.

Tara, Emily and Kate shuffled through the door with the rest of the crowd and were swept along a corridor. Tara hoped they were going the right way. She looked at the map again. There was no time to worry about Sam now. It was going to take all of her brainpower just to find her next classroom.

Chapter Five

Tara couldn't stop thinking about the competition. The most thrilling day of her life was only two months away! Of course, there was a lot of hard work to get through first. Clare had asked the ten Silverdale gymnasts competing at the Regionals to come for extra practice sessions on Sundays, as well as the three training sessions they already did with the rest of the group.

Today was their first Sunday session. After the

warm-up, Clare told them she would work with each pair or group separately, while the others could get on with practising by themselves. The coach had started teaching each pair their routines for the competition earlier in the week, and Tara already loved going through the sequence of moves closely with Lindsay and Clare, knowing that their coach had created it especially for them. Tara and Lindsay were working harder than ever, trying to get to grips with the beginning section of the routine. They were getting much better at front angel too. And there were other balances to start on. Clare left them practising a new one, and went to work with Jasmine and Sam.

"Shall we just practise front angel again?" Lindsay suggested, after they'd tried and tried and *tried* to get their newest balance right. They were learning a variation on the standing-on-shoulders balance that now came easily to them. Tara was supposed to stand on Lindsay's shoulders, like she'd learned to do for the summer display, but now Clare wanted her to lift one leg in the air in a Y-balance while she was up there.

"No," breathed Tara, gasping for air on the floor where she'd landed. "We can do front angel now. This is the one that needs work."

Lindsay sighed. "I know. But it's so hard!"

"That's why we need to keep trying," Tara insisted. She got up and stood facing Lindsay. She glanced at Sam and Jasmine, who were working with Clare. They were competing in a higher level, and their routine was packed with difficult and impressive balances. "I bet Sam and Jas could do this balance easy-peasy."

That did it. Lindsay looked at them and then back at her partner. "Come on, then. What are you waiting for?"

Tara grinned. Ever since Sam had been so nasty in the changing room, Lindsay had been just as determined as Tara that they would win their level at Regionals. Whenever Tara showed signs of getting tired or frustrated, Lindsay reminded her that they were going to prove Sam wrong.

Tara climbed up to stand on Lindsay's shoulders. When she was balancing steadily, Lindsay let go of Tara's right leg, and Tara lifted it up by grabbing hold of the heel of her foot, and tried to straighten her leg so that her toes were pointing towards the ceiling. She raised her left arm up to the side, too, so that her body made a Y position. Her right leg was almost straight when she began tipping over to the side. There was nothing Lindsay could do to stop her. Tara landed – crash, splat – on the squashy blue mat. Again. She was glad Sam was busy working with Clare – she hoped the older gymnast hadn't seen how many times she'd fallen today. She looked up to see Lindsay's face peering down at her. "Front angel?"

Tara was frustrated, but one of the things she loved most about gymnastics was the fact that there was always something new to learn. You worked for ages and ages on something, and as soon as you got it right, all you wanted was to master the next skill. Still, it did feel wonderful when you could perform something well...

Balancing horizontally in the air on Lindsay's up-stretched hands, Tara smiled. Megan, coming down neatly from a balance with Sophie, gave her a grin and a thumbs up. "Great front angel, Tara!" she called.

Tara smiled but when she landed tidily on the floor, the wonderful feeling of flying was gone. It was time to get back to work on the balance they couldn't do.

At home that afternoon, Tara got out her school bag so that she could finish the homework she needed to do for Monday. But she kept getting distracted and, instead of doing her homework, she practised Y-balances wherever she could. She did them standing on the floor (which was easy), standing on the bed (which was less easy) and even one on the arm of the sofa (which was really not easy, and ended with a telling-off and a frightened cat). She was balancing in her bedroom when the pop song she'd chosen as her mobile phone ringtone interrupted her.

Tara jumped off her bed and grabbed her phone from the bedside table. It was Emily. Tara couldn't wait to tell her about the special training session.

"Are you coming round?" Emily asked. "Kate's on her way, she's bringing a couple of DVDs she got yesterday."

Tara looked at her watch. It was nearly four o'clock already. "Oh, no, I can't," she replied. "I've got to finish my homework for tomorrow."

"But we haven't seen each other all weekend," said Emily.

"I know," Tara said, cringing. Last year the three friends had started watching films together early on Sunday evenings. They hadn't bothered much about it in the summer holidays, because they could do things together any time they wanted.

But when they'd realized that they would be split up for most of the day at school this year, they'd all agreed that seeing each other on Sunday evenings was even more important. How could she have forgotten already? They usually only missed it for really important things like family birthdays or when they were ill. "It's just that I had gym this morning, and yesterday too, so I haven't had time to get it all done," she said. "I'm really sorry, Em."

"Oh," said Emily. And then after a second, "That's okay. You're probably really tired, anyway. I'm exhausted, and I'm not the one who's been doing gym all weekend!"

"I am tired," Tara admitted. "Lindsay and I are working *so* hard at the moment." She rubbed her shoulder where she'd knocked it a few times at the gym. "And you know how tiring school is. But next week, I promise I'll be there!"

"Okay," said Emily. She paused, like she was trying to think of something to say. "Well, see you tomorrow."

"Yeah," said Tara. "Bye."

She put the phone down, then dragged her school bag downstairs to the kitchen table and got on with her homework. But all evening she was distracted, thinking about Kate and Emily, wondering what DVD they were watching and what they were talking about. She felt left out, knowing that they were watching a Sunday evening film and she wasn't with them.

When she went to bed that night, she thought about gymnastics, going through balances and throws in her head. But Kate and Emily still kept popping into her mind. For once, she wanted it to be time for school so that she could see her friends.

Chapter Six

Tara met Kate and Emily at the school gate the
next morning. Kate told her all about the film
they'd watched. It sounded great and Tara wished
she'd been there.

"We'll watch it again another weekend," Emily
said generously.

"Definitely," Kate agreed. "You have to see it,
Tara! Then we can all watch the second one." The
bell rang, and they hurried off to their form rooms.

✳ ✳ ✳

After registration, Tara found Emily on the way to the science block. Even though they'd met at the gate that morning, Tara felt like they had loads to catch up on. And by the time they met Kate on the field at break time, after Tara and Emily had spent a whole science lesson sitting next to each other, they still had lots to talk about. They chatted and laughed, all three at once, as if they hadn't seen each other for months.

When the bell rang, they headed back towards the main building. The end of break time was always chaos. Girls and boys suddenly swarmed towards classrooms, calling and shouting to each other, and running down the corridors (even though it wasn't allowed). The three friends were just about to turn the corner towards their maths classroom when Tara heard someone calling her name.

She turned around. "Hi, Lindsay!" Kate and Emily stopped too, a little behind Tara.

"I've been thinking about that balance," Lindsay began.

"I've been practising Y-balances non-stop," said Tara.

"That's good," Lindsay said. "But I think I know where we're going wrong." Lindsay tried to explain, while people pushed past them on the way to lessons, but she couldn't get the words right.

"Tara, we've got to go," Kate said, crossing her arms. "Break's over. We'll get in trouble."

"One minute," said Tara. She was desperate to see if she and Lindsay could fix the balance.

"Come on, Tara," insisted Kate.

"I'll ask Miss Isaac if we can use the gym sometime to practise," said Lindsay.

"I'm sorry...but I'm going," said Kate, and rushed off. Emily followed hesitantly, then hurried to catch up. They disappeared in the mass of blue and grey.

"That would be amazing." Tara grinned at

Lindsay. The corridor was starting to become empty. "See you on Wednesday," she said quickly, and then ran to the maths classroom. She was late. Mr. Spencer gave her an annoyed look as she sat down, but Tara was thinking of that massive gym where they'd had PE on the first day of term. The thought of practising gymnastics in there filled her stomach with butterflies. A whole gym for just two of them... She hoped Miss Isaac said yes.

Tara kept an eye out for Lindsay at lunchtime, but she couldn't see her anywhere. She didn't see her at the end of the day either, or when she arrived at school the next morning. At the end of Tuesday break, she dawdled behind her friends on the way back inside. She'd just given up and was running to catch up with them when she heard Lindsay calling her.

"I asked Miss Isaac," Lindsay panted, out of breath from her dash to catch Tara. "She said we can use the gym at lunchtimes as long as we don't touch any equipment and use crash mats if we're trying anything difficult."

"Brilliant!" whooped Tara.

"What's happening?" demanded Kate.

"Lindsay and I are allowed to use the gym to practise our balances."

"When?" asked Emily.

"Lunchtimes," Tara replied. "Every lunchtime, if we want." She waved to Lindsay and trooped inside with the others. "We won't get that long in there, once we've had lunch and warmed up, but it means we can practise every day. And we really need to if we're going to win that competition."

"That's good," said Emily. "It's really nice of Miss Isaac to let you."

"Great," agreed Kate, "as long as you don't forget about us! At this rate the only time we'll ever see you will be to play netball once a week, or to talk about fractions."

Tara laughed. "Don't be silly," she said, linking

her arm through Kate's. "Anyway, it's just until the competition."

Kate pulled away when they reached her English classroom. "See you later," she said, and disappeared through the door, while Tara and Emily turned in opposite directions for their next lessons.

Chapter Seven

The next day, Tara queued up for lunch with her friends as usual. They found a space at the end of one of the long tables and sat down; Kate and Emily chatted while Tara rushed through her meal. When she'd finished eating, she stood and picked up her tray.

"See you later," she said.

"Where are you going?" Kate asked.

"I'm going to practise gym with Lindsay,"

Tara reminded her.

"But aren't you coming outside with us?"

"Sorry," Tara said. "Linds got the gym for us, and we really need to practise."

"Oh, okay," said Kate. "Have a good time!"

In the gym, Tara and Lindsay quickly laid down a few of the thin mats on the hard floor. They did a bit of a warm-up and then started to work on balances. They went through the beginning of their routine, which was all they knew so far, counting the beats out loud or in their heads because they didn't have the music. Tara practised standing on Lindsay's shoulders with one leg stretched out behind her in an arabesque. It was easier than the Y-balance and it helped her get used to balancing up there on one leg.

Every lunchtime was the same; Tara ate lunch with her two best friends as fast as she could, then dashed off to change into her PE kit and meet Lindsay in the gym. By the end of the second week, when Tara gulped down her food and got up from the table, Kate didn't even react.

On Sunday evening they watched a DVD at Tara's house and everything seemed normal but on Monday, when Tara got to their usual lunchtime meeting place, Kate and Emily weren't there. She waited, thinking that they'd probably got held up in their art lesson, which they had together. Five minutes ticked by. Tara kept looking despairingly at her watch. She was losing precious training time! There was still no sign of her friends, so she slipped into the lunch queue by herself. After getting some food, she walked nervously towards the tables. Suddenly, eating lunch by herself seemed pretty scary. Was everyone going to think she had no friends? Where was the best place to attract the least attention sitting alone? Then she spotted Lindsay and Megan having lunch with some of the other Year Nines. Relieved, she headed for their table, where she could see an empty seat next to Lindsay.

"This is Tara, my Acro partner," Lindsay said, introducing her to the other girls at the table.

"Hi," she said shyly. Megan reeled off the names of the other girls, and Tara smiled at them all.

"You should come to the gym and practise with us!" Tara suggested to Megan.

"Thanks," said Megan. "Lindsay asked me the other week. But there's not much point without Sophie."

"True." Tara nodded, thinking that she was lucky her partner was at the same school. Sophie went to a different school, with Jasmine and Sam and some of the boys.

Tara felt shy, so she kept quiet and ate quickly to catch up with Lindsay. She listened to the others' conversation; they seemed funny and kind, and by the time she'd finished eating, she didn't feel quite so intimidated. As she and Lindsay went out of the hall, she saw Kate and Emily sitting at a table at the other end of the room. She hadn't even noticed them come in and she felt a bit guilty that she'd been having lunch with Lindsay and Megan when she could have been chatting to her best friends.

Soon Tara and Lindsay had the opening section of their routine absolutely perfect and the Y-balance was getting much better. Sometimes they spent a while working on things like walkovers, handsprings and long, steady handstands as well. Tara knew that if she and Lindsay were ever going to be able to do the most difficult balances, she'd have to be able to hold a handstand as steady as a house. Tara was desperate to work on backflips, too. Lindsay could do them, but Tara could only manage with support from Clare and she felt bad that they couldn't put one in their routine. She was sure that if she was just brave enough to try on her own, she'd be able to do it. But in the school gym, without her coach, she was afraid of hurting herself. An injury would put her out of training for a while and, even worse, out of the competition. It wasn't worth it. But one day soon...

They continued to work on their routine with Clare at Silverdale too, of course, and the coach seemed pleased with their progress. It wasn't long before they'd learned the whole thing. Clare had chosen a piece of upbeat, jazzy music, which made Tara feel light and happy every time she heard it. Their coach had choreographed a routine to match – it was full of bouncy jumps and turns, and the gymnasts had to be very light on their feet. Their split leaps and handsprings went perfectly with the music, and the balances were in just the right places to work as well. The balances were slowly improving, but every time they saw Jasmine and Sam doing a perfect one, they knew they needed to work harder. Even though they weren't competing against them, they wanted their simpler balances to look just as perfect as the older pair's more difficult ones.

After three weeks of practising at lunchtime as

well as at Silverdale, Tara felt like front angel came as easily to them as a cartwheel and the difficult Y-balance on Lindsay's shoulder was almost perfect.

"You two have really improved!" Clare said, when she saw them practising at the gym.

"We've been working on the routine at lunchtime at school," explained Lindsay.

"Keep it up," said Clare, "and soon every second of it will be beautiful and faultless."

Tara and Lindsay grinned at each other – impressing Clare made the hard work worth it.

As the weeks flew by, the competition was getting closer and Tara realized she was seeing less and less of Emily and Kate. She had lunch with Lindsay and Megan and their friends a couple of days a week because Kate and Emily always seemed to be running late, and she hadn't seen them for a Sunday evening film for ages and ages. There was always homework to do after gym at the weekends, and by the time six o'clock came she was usually half-asleep already. She missed them, but she and Lindsay were getting better and better with every practice, and Clare seemed to think they were doing well, so she kept telling herself that it was worth it and she'd make it up to her friends once the competition was over.

"Tara," said Kate, grabbing her arm on their way out of the maths classroom one Tuesday morning, "we're going to the Sixth Form fashion show at lunchtime, d'you want to come?"

"When did you decide that?" asked Tara.

"We saw the poster last week," said Emily. "It's for charity."

"You're never around at lunchtimes, and we hardly ever get to talk in lessons. We haven't even seen you at break time this week!" said Kate. "I was going to ask you about it this morning but you weren't at the gate."

"I overslept," said Tara. "I only just got here in time for registration." She had tried and tried to find her friends at break time today and yesterday, but they hadn't been at their usual meeting place outside because it had been raining. They weren't allowed to have mobile phones in school so she hadn't even been able to text them to ask where they were.

"So are you coming to the fashion show?" asked Emily.

"I don't think I can," said Tara. "I mean… Lindsay and I really need to keep practising for the competition."

Emily looked disappointed, Tara noticed, but Kate rolled her eyes.

"Never mind," said Kate, and she strode off down the corridor towards her next lesson.

Emily looked at Tara, as if to say *You know what Kate's like*, and gave her a half-smile, but as they walked to the science block in silence, Tara wished there was something she could do to make things better with her friends.

Chapter Eight

"**Y**our turn, Tara!" Megan gave her a little shove in the back.

"Oh!" Tara broke off from her conversation with Jasmine and Sophie and stepped forward. They were in the middle of one of their usual after-school Wednesday training sessions. The gymnasts who weren't competing at Regionals were there too, so they were spending the first half of the session working on tumbling and individual skills.

Friendships and Backflips

Tara stared down the tumbling track to the foam pit at the end. A mat for landings had been placed on top of the foam blocks. Tara pointed one foot forward, took a deep breath, and ran. At the end of the track she jumped onto both feet, and pushed up and over into a front somersault. She landed on her bum and sighed. She could do somersaults on the trampoline really well now and she'd hoped that doing them on the track wouldn't be too much harder.

"You're not getting enough height," Clare said, as Tara had known she would. "You need to jump *up* first, and then tuck round." Tara nodded and jogged back to join the end of the line again. Not wanting to waste any time, she practised jumping as high as she could on the track. She realized how much she'd been relying on the bounce of the trampoline to get her up into the air. When she looked up again, Jasmine was performing a perfect tumble run – round-off, flick, straight back somersault. Tara closed her eyes and imagined herself doing that.

"Wakey-wakey!" she heard someone say behind her. She opened her eyes with a start and blushed. It was Sam. Tara smiled uncertainly at her and bounced a few steps along the track to catch up to her place in the queue. It was nearly her turn again. This time, as she ran, she thought *height, height, height* all the way along the track, and when she got to the end, she flew up higher than she ever thought she could. Her body spun round in a tucked position and her feet shot out just in time for her to land on them. She wobbled forward a little, but tightened all her muscles and held onto her standing position.

"Brilliant!" cried Clare. Tara glowed with delight. She could hardly believe she'd managed the landing. She bounded back to the line with a huge smile on her face.

"Did you see that?" she squealed, high-fiving Jasmine and Megan at the same time. They nodded enthusiastically.

"Awesome," said Megan.

"I can't wait to go again," Tara gushed.

"It's addictive," agreed Lindsay. "When I first managed it, I felt like I never wanted to do anything else."

"I want to do *everything* else!" exclaimed Tara, and she laughed excitedly.

The others laughed, too. "Do another one like that first," Jasmine said, smiling, and then stepped forward for her turn.

"It was probably a fluke," Tara said to Lindsay and Megan.

"No way," said Megan.

"We'll see," muttered Sam, standing behind them.

By the time they finished on the track, Tara had ended another two somersaults sitting on the mat, but had landed one more on her feet. The landing might not have been perfect, but she was just happy to be standing up.

✱ ✱ ✱

Later, while Tara was holding a steady front angel above Lindsay's head, she looked around at the rest of the gym. One of the things that she really liked about the Wednesday afternoon training sessions was that they used the gym at the same time as the more advanced Acro squad. They were in training for international competitions and some of them were already World Champions. Tara loved stealing glances at them while she warmed up, or when she was doing an easy balance. She often saw Jasmine watching them too, and guessed that her friend had set her heart on being part of that group someday.

Lindsay brought Tara down from front angel and back to reality. She took another quick look at the advanced group and made a promise to herself that she would be one of them in a few years. The Regional competition was the first step on the way.

"Do you think they ever struggled with the kind of balances we're doing?" Tara asked

Lindsay, tilting her head towards the advanced group on the other floor area.

"Of course," said Lindsay. "Steph used to be in this group – she started here the same time as me and she found things hard just like everyone else."

"How did she get into that group?"

Lindsay shrugged. "Partly luck. They needed a new base and she was the right height. If they'd wanted a small gymnast to be a top in balances, it would've been Jasmine. But Steph's good, and she always works really hard. They notice that sort of thing."

Tara nodded. She could do the hard work part. Maybe if she crossed her fingers and used all her birthday cake wishes for the next few years, someone else would take care of the luck.

"Let's get back to work," said Tara. "Do you want to go through the whole routine, or just balances again?"

"Have you got plans to move group, then?" teased Lindsay with a knowing smile.

"Not just yet," said Tara. She grinned. "Let's win this competition first."

Clare asked Tara to stay behind at the end of training. As she sat down on the floor and waited for Clare to finish chatting to another coach, Tara watched her group disappear into the lobby, and felt her stomach plummet down to the springy floor. What did Clare want to talk to her about? Had she done something wrong? Maybe Clare had decided to pull her out of the competition...but then wouldn't she have kept Lindsay back too?

The advanced group still had another half an hour of training and Tara watched Steph and her partner enviously as they performed neat backflips followed by back somersaults, perfectly in time with each other. She *wished* that she could do a backflip so easily. With all the practice for the competition, she hadn't had a chance to work on them for a while.

"Sorry to keep you waiting, Tara," Clare said, coming back to the floor.

Tara got to her feet nervously. "Is something the matter?" she asked.

Clare smiled. "Don't look so worried! You're not in trouble. Come with me." She turned and walked towards the door. Tara followed her coach out to the lobby and into the gym club's small office. She looked around at the cluttered shelves and the desk piled high with folders, pieces of paper, water bottles and lunch boxes that had been left behind. She'd never really thought about this side of the gym; she'd had no idea that so much went on behind the scenes of coaching and competing. Just like in the lobby, there were lots of photographs on the walls – old Summer Display pictures, and more photos of gymnasts holding up trophies and medals. There was a beautiful framed poster of an Acrobatic Gymnastics mixed pair too. The boy was holding the girl high above his head; she was standing on his hands, balancing on one foot. She was holding the other foot up behind her to touch her head. Tara gazed at the image in awe.

Clare smiled, seeing her expression. "That was a long time ago," she said. "They were one of the best pairs we've ever had here. They won every competition going, when they were at their best."

"Wow," breathed Tara.

Clare let Tara look at the poster for a few more seconds. "Now," she said. "I asked you to stay behind because we need to get you sorted out with a leotard and tracksuit for the competition."

Tara's entire face lit up. One of the things she'd noticed about the photos in the lobby was that a lot of the gymnasts who'd won competitions were wearing the same leotard. She couldn't wait to have one of her own; an official Silverdale leotard.

Clare pulled a box out from under the desk. She rummaged around, and handed Tara a leotard folded and wrapped in plastic. Then she pulled out a bigger package that contained the tracksuit. Lindsay and the others in her group often wore their Silverdale tracksuits to keep warm at the beginning of training.

"Go and try these on," said Clare.

Tara didn't need telling twice. She beamed, then skipped out of the office and into the changing room.

The leotard fitted perfectly. It felt as if it had been made especially for her. She looked in the mirror. The Silverdale squad leotards were sleeveless and velvety; dark blue with a white flame that licked down diagonally from the right shoulder. Only gymnasts who competed were allowed to wear them. She tried the tracksuit on too. It was also navy blue and white, and said *Silverdale Gymnastics Club* on the back in white letters. It fitted well.

Tara hugged her arms around herself with excitement. She couldn't wait until the competition, when she could wear the leotard and tracksuit for real as part of the Silverdale team. With only three weeks to go, it suddenly felt a lot closer.

Chapter Nine

"I've just had the best idea!" Kate said on the first Sunday of half-term. She was sitting on the floor of her bedroom with her back against the end of her pink and white bed. She tilted her head backwards to look at Emily and Tara, who were lying on their stomachs, side by side on the bed. They were watching a film they'd all seen before, so they were talking over most of it. Tara was tired from a hard session at the gym that morning, but she was so happy to finally be watching a DVD on a Sunday evening with her friends. She felt like she hadn't seen Emily and Kate for ages and she really missed them. Half-term meant that homework could wait. Tonight was all about films, fun and friendship.

Kate turned to announce her plan. "Do you guys want to go ice skating tomorrow?"

"Can't," said Tara. "I've got gym."

"But it's half-term!" moaned Kate. "We've survived almost two months of Year Seven, now we need to have some *fun*. Don't you get *any* holidays?"

"No. We have extra training for the competition instead," Tara replied. "I don't want holidays from gym, anyway. The extra sessions are great. Megan did the funniest impression of Clare the other day!"

"Can't we go in the morning, before gym?" suggested Emily.

"Not really," Tara said. She was trying to see if she could lift one leg behind her and touch her foot to her head without raising herself up. She stopped for a moment and reached for a handful of popcorn from the bowl next to Kate. "I've spent so much time training for Regionals that I'm really behind on homework. I haven't even started my art project yet."

"Why don't you come round to mine another day and we can all do our homework together?" said Emily. "Do you have to do a talk about something important in history? We've all got different teachers, so Kate and I thought we could all pick the same topic and do the research together."

"We were thinking of doing the Great Fire of London – something really dramatic," added Kate.

"Oh, well…" Tara mumbled, wondering when they had made all these decisions. "I kind of wanted to do mine about the history of the Olympics."

Kate rolled her eyes. "Let me guess: so you can talk lots about gymnastics?"

"Mr. Bruce *did* say we should choose something we're interested in," Tara said, trying to defend herself, but Kate sighed loudly and angrily.

"All you care about is gymnastics!" she said.

"That's not true!" Tara sat up on the bed. "It just takes up a lot of time…"

"Yeah, we know *that*. We never see you any more! And when we do see you, it's all you ever talk about!" Suddenly Kate was almost shouting. "You're always talking about your Silverdale friends – it's like you don't want to be friends with *us* any more."

"Kate, stop it…" Emily said quietly.

But Kate was too angry to stop. "It's always 'Lindsay this' and 'Megan said that' and I'm sick of it. I wish you'd stop being so *boring*!"

Tara stared at Kate. She couldn't believe what her friend was saying. "I do want to see you! There's just so much to fit in… I'm so sorry, I didn't know I was being like that…" She couldn't say anything more; she had started to cry. She was so tired. With school and gym and homework, she felt like she hadn't stopped for a rest for *months*. She didn't get to see Emily and Kate as much now that they were all in different classes at school, but that didn't mean that she didn't like them any more! Earlier, she'd felt so relieved that she could finally spend some time with her best friends, but now everything was getting ruined.

Kate looked shocked. "Tara," she said, her voice softening. "I'm sorry. I didn't mean to upset you."

Emily put her arm around Tara's shoulders. "Don't cry," she said. "You've got so much going on, and it must be so exciting...just don't forget the people who've been your friends since nursery, okay?"

"I haven't forgotten!" cried Tara. "You two are my best friends ever! It's just...I've been desperate to do gym for so long, and I'm so excited about it that I wanted to share it with you guys... I promise I won't go on about it any more though."

"And if you do, we'll tell you to shut up, alright?" Kate grinned. Tara laughed and nodded. "Sorry, Tara," said Kate. She scrambled up onto the bed and put her arm around her friend from the other side.

"Friends?" asked Tara.

"*Best* friends," Kate said firmly, with a nod. Then she reached out and put her other arm around Emily, squeezing the three of them tightly together. They collapsed onto the bed, giggling and gasping for air.

"So I guess you're too busy to do anything tomorrow?" Kate asked later, while Tara was tying the laces on her pink Converse trainers. Mum was chatting to Kate's parents in the kitchen. Emily's dad had picked her up ten minutes ago.

"Yeah," said Tara. "Sorry."

Kate sighed. "It's alright." She shrugged. "The competition's important to you. I know that."

But Tara knew Kate as well as she knew her

own family. She could tell it wasn't alright really. She hugged Kate tightly when she left, trying to show her that they were still best friends. It was the only way she could think of.

On the way home in the car with Mum, she stared silently out of the window.

"Have you and Kate fallen out?" Mum asked, as if she could read Tara's mind.

"She's upset that I'm spending so much time doing gym," said Tara. "She thinks I don't want to be her friend any more." Her voice wobbled as she spoke and she felt like she was going to cry again. "Mum, what should I do? I miss Kate and Em, and I feel like I hardly ever see them now, but Clare said we had to be one hundred per cent committed to the competition."

"I don't know," said Mum. "What do you think Clare meant by that?"

"Well, she meant that we have to go to every training session and work hard, and that we should put the competition first... And I thought that meant we should practise by ourselves as well as at Silverdale, but now I'm not sure. Perhaps I'm doing too much… I just don't know."

She'd thought of another way to show Kate and Emily that she still cared about them, but she wasn't sure if she was prepared to do it. Cutting back on gymnastics training would definitely save her friendships…but it might also mean giving up her shot at a gold medal, her chance to prove Sam wrong, and her first opportunity to show everyone at Silverdale that she was going to go far. Hard work was going to get her into the advanced group one day.

"I don't know what to do!" she said, looking desperately at Mum for an answer. "If I stop doing all the extra practice with Lindsay, will I be throwing away my chance of getting to Nationals? And if I *don't* stop, will I lose my friends?"

Chapter Ten

There was extra training for the competition on Monday, and then a family visit to Auntie Hazel on Tuesday. The Wednesday afternoon training session came around and Tara hadn't been in touch with Kate or Emily at all. She still hadn't started her homework either, she remembered, which would take up at least another day. When had life got so busy? To push away her worries, she threw herself into practising with Lindsay.

"How about the Regionals gymnasts show us their routines?" Clare suggested to the group, when they were coming up to the end of the regular training session.

There were eager yeses from everyone. Tara and Lindsay's routine was so much better now that they were practising at school, and she was really proud of it. She couldn't wait to show the others. The gymnasts settled down at the edge of the floor area to watch.

The group of four boys went first. Tara found their routine exciting – they did balances she'd never even imagined, and their perfectly timed round-off flicks looked great. Because there were four of them, they could perform human pyramids and other balances that were three people high. Jack, who was at the top of all these balances, fearlessly climbed up to stand on Dom's shoulders, while Dom balanced on the thighs of the two strongest boys.

Sam and Jasmine went next – they had a great

routine, and Tara could tell they stood a good chance of winning the Level 4 competition. Tiny Jasmine held handstands on Sam's hands, was thrown over in somersaults and showed amazing flexibility. Sam lifted her up as if she was a doll. They performed to a piece of beautiful classical music that built up to an explosion of sound as Sam threw Jasmine high into a double somersault at the end.

"They're so good!" Tara whispered to Megan.

"Sickening, isn't it?" Megan replied.

But Megan and Sophie were good, too. Their routine wasn't as difficult and impressive as Sam and Jasmine's but they did their balances well and had a great rhythm that was fun to watch. Megan was a born performer, and she charmed the small audience with her smile, packing loads of personality into the routine alongside backflips, jumps and turns.

Tara and Lindsay went last. Now that she'd seen the others' routines, Tara felt nervous. She and

Lindsay were competing in a lower level, so they weren't expected to do such difficult balances. But she wasn't sure that they even performed their simple balances as perfectly as the others did theirs.

As they began the routine, Tara tried to push away the thought that everyone was watching... that Sam was just waiting for her to make a mistake. And everything went well until they got to the Y-balance on Lindsay's shoulders. They were facing their audience, and Tara caught Sam's eye. She couldn't tell what the older girl was thinking, but Sam was looking at her very critically. Tara had just straightened her leg up to the side, and she hoped Sam might be impressed, but the older girl's expression didn't change. Distracted, Tara lost her balance just for a moment – but a moment was enough. As she tilted over to the side, she could do nothing to stop herself from falling. She crashed to the mat.

Tara got to her feet, burning bright red, and

almost cried. None of the others had fallen from a balance. Sam was right – she was going to let Silverdale down. She wanted to run out of the gym, run all the way home and hide in her bed for ever, but she knew they had to finish the routine. Clare had told them again and again how important it was to keep going if they made a mistake. They performed the last moves well enough, but Tara hardly cared. She wasn't as good as the others. They weren't going to win.

Sam exchanged a look with Mel. She didn't say anything, but Tara didn't need her to. This time, she knew exactly what Sam was thinking.

Tara felt sick as she sat back down with the others. What would Clare say about her terrible mistake? There were two weeks left until Regionals and it had all gone wrong.

"Don't worry so much," said the coach, when she saw Tara's miserable expression. "Everyone has bad days. I know you can do the balance better than that."

Behind her, Sam raised an eyebrow at Tara, then turned and walked off to the changing room.

Tara couldn't stop worrying. On Friday morning she went shopping with Kate as Emily's birthday was coming up and they both wanted to find the perfect present for her. Falling from the balance was still on Tara's mind, and she really wanted to talk to Kate about it. But after the argument they'd had at the beginning of half-term, she thought it was best to keep her mouth shut about gymnastics – Kate didn't want to hear it. And the last thing Tara wanted was another fight. She just wished everything could go back to how it was before. It felt horrible to keep her worries about Sam and the balance to herself. She felt like she was keeping a big secret from one of the people who knew her better than anyone.

They wandered around the shops until Tara had to leave, but they had no luck with finding gifts for Emily.

Friendships and Backflips

"We'll just have to go shopping separately, whenever we have time," sighed Kate. "I can go tomorrow morning but, of course, you have gym then."

Tara felt Kate's words prickling her but she *couldn't* miss a training session, not after what had happened at the last one. She needed the practice now more than ever, no matter how much she missed her friends.

Chapter Eleven

Tara arrived at the gym that afternoon determined to make up for Wednesday's mistake. She changed into her black and silver leotard and sat down on a bench in the changing room, waiting for Lindsay and the others. Then she leaned back against the wall and closed her eyes. She was so tired. She'd hardly slept the last two nights because she was worrying about the balance going wrong again. Shopping with Kate had been fun, but they'd spent almost the whole day walking around the big shopping centre in the middle of town. Her legs felt worn out.

When the others arrived and the training session got started she pulled herself together and after a vigorous warm-up, she felt ready to work harder than ever. Tara and Lindsay tried and tried to get the Y-balance working again...but it was no good. The harder they tried, the worse the balance got. After about an hour, Clare came up to them and asked them to go through their routine. When they got to the difficult standing-on-shoulders Y-balance, Tara wobbled and fell. She knew she was tired, but the problem was bigger than that – the balance felt completely gone, as if they'd never been able to do it at all.

"Tara! What is the matter with you?" shouted Clare. Everyone stopped what they were doing, and looked at them. Their coach rarely shouted. "Lindsay? I know it's half-term and you're on holiday from school, but you need to take this seriously." Lindsay and Tara nodded, but said nothing. "Again, please. I want to see you do that balance properly."

They tried again. If Tara hadn't already been red-faced from the exercise, she would definitely have been pink with shame. She bit her lip hard and hoped that she wouldn't cry. They managed to hold the balance this time, but not very steadily. As Tara jumped down she heard Sam mutter, "It's not like it's difficult. I guess this is what you get when you let a *new girl* compete."

"Work on it," Clare said. She looked so cross with them that Tara couldn't meet her eyes. She wondered if her coach agreed with Sam. Did *everyone* think she was going to let the club down?

She hardly spoke to anyone for the last half an hour. She was afraid that if she did, she would melt into a mess of childish tears. Lindsay was quiet too, but then she always was. Tara held on until they'd got changed and she and Lindsay were walking out to the car park. Once they were outside, Tara allowed the tears to roll down her flushed cheeks.

"Hey, don't cry," said Lindsay gently. "Clare won't be angry any more by tomorrow."

"It's not that," sniffed Tara. "It's...what are we going to do?"

"Get better at it, I suppose," replied Lindsay.

"I don't see how!" cried Tara. "We're already practising every day at school as well as here. What more can we do? Maybe I'm just not good enough to be a gymnast." But the thought of not doing gym filled her with horror. "Oh, but I *have* to be!"

"You could come round to my house after training tomorrow," Lindsay offered. "We can work on our balances all afternoon. We'll get lots more done without the others, and we'll have more time than we do at school."

Tara blinked away some tears and looked up at her, amazed. Doing even more extra practice was such an obvious idea, but only someone as calm as Lindsay would be able to think of it in the middle of such a crisis.

They managed to get through training the next morning without making Clare angry again and by the time they got back to Lindsay's house afterwards, Tara was already feeling better. She looked around. The living room was comfortable and tidy. There wasn't any of the clutter that seemed almost part of the decoration in Tara's home. But she did spot a pair of ballet shoes tucked away in one corner.

"Do you do ballet as well as gym?" she asked, knowing that Lindsay didn't have any sisters or brothers who the shoes might belong to.

"Yeah," Lindsay replied, frowning slightly. "Please don't tell Clare though. We're not supposed to do ballet because it works your muscles in a different way."

"I won't tell," Tara promised worriedly. She

didn't want Lindsay to get in any more trouble with their coach, but she couldn't help feeling anxious that Lindsay was doing something she wasn't really allowed to. And what about the one hundred per cent commitment that Clare wanted? Didn't doing other things take Lindsay's focus away from gymnastics? "Have you kept it a secret the whole time you've been at Silverdale?"

"No. When I first started Acro I was already doing ballet. It was fine for a few years, but when I was put into Clare's group and started competing, Clare said it would be a good idea to stop ballet. I did stop, but then about a year ago Clare organized a one-off ballet class to help us be more graceful and elegant when we perform. I realized how much I missed it, so I started classes again. Just twice a week. I hate lying to Clare, but I know she'd make me stop."

"Don't you worry that it will interfere with your Acro training? I mean…if Clare said it's not good to do both, that must be true."

"I do worry about that sometimes," said Lindsay. "I really do love gym. But I love ballet as well. We spend so much time training at Silverdale. We should be allowed to have other interests too."

Tara nodded thoughtfully. She couldn't think of anything to say. Lindsay still looked very serious.

"Shall we make some lunch?" offered Lindsay, suddenly changing the subject. "And then we can get to work."

They ate cheese sandwiches at the kitchen table with Lindsay's mum and then went upstairs to Lindsay's bedroom. Her room was fairly big, and covered from floor to ceiling with posters and pictures of ballet dancers and gymnasts. A few gymnastics medals hung from the bedpost at the end of her bed. Tara stared at the walls. She'd had no idea Lindsay was such a ballet fanatic!

On the bookshelf were some framed photos of Lindsay in different costumes. In one of them she was a cute little girl – maybe only five or six years old – wearing a little white tutu and holding up a wand with a silver star on the top. She was smiling in a way Tara had never seen the teenager Lindsay smile in the gym. It reminded Tara of the way she herself had looked in the photos Dad took of the Silverdale Summer Display.

"I'm just a *little* bit obsessed. Maybe," joked Lindsay.

"This is why you're always so calm about the gym competition."

Lindsay nodded. "It's not that I don't care…I do. It's just not *everything* to me."

"It's everything to me," replied Tara.

"It doesn't have to be. I love Acro, but I need other things to take my mind off it sometimes. When things go wrong or I'm worrying about a balance, I think about ballet instead and then I realize that gym isn't the only thing in the world. Gymnastics can't be the only thing you care about. You'd go mad."

Even though it was the beginning of November, the sky was clear, with brilliant sunshine. They had both put long-sleeved tops and their Silverdale tracksuit trousers on over their leotards at the end of their training session, and once they'd warmed up properly in Lindsay's bedroom, they were not too cold to practise outside. Lindsay's garden was small, but they had enough space to work on balances, even if they couldn't fit in the whole routine. All afternoon, they worked on standing on shoulders and their other balances. They didn't fall from balances or try anything dangerous, so it didn't matter that there weren't any mats. By five o'clock they were worn out, but pleased with how they were getting on.

Tara thought about Lindsay's ballet bedroom all evening, and remembered what her partner had said. Was she right? Was gymnastics going to take over her whole world until there was nothing left? At Lindsay's house they'd worked hard, but they'd also chatted and laughed and had a lot of fun.

For that afternoon they were simply two friends doing gymnastics together because they enjoyed it, instead of serious gymnasts training for a competition. Maybe being more relaxed had helped them to hold their balances better, Tara thought. It was hard to balance when all you could think about was how terrible it would be if you didn't.

She was starting to realize something else, too: being with Lindsay and her other friends was one of the things she loved most about Silverdale. Without them, gym wouldn't be as much fun. And without Emily and Kate, school – no, *life* – would be unbearable.

"Morning, girls!" Clare called from the office, as Tara and Megan hurried to the changing room on Sunday morning.

"Lindsay and I have been practising *loads*," Tara said earnestly.

"Great," replied Clare. "I'll look forward to seeing your routine today, then."

When they did show their coach their routine, Tara wasn't worried at all. She and Lindsay had managed to get their balances almost perfect when they practised in the garden. Doing them in the gym would be just the same. As they moved through the familiar steps and balances, Tara pretended that she was at Lindsay's house, and that it was just the two of them, with no pressure to get it perfect, and no one to judge them. It worked.

"Much better!" cried Clare, when they finished. She even clapped. "You actually looked like you were enjoying yourselves. I don't know what's happened since Friday, but you two have made a real improvement. Listen, you're a new pair and I took a risk entering you in this competition but I honestly think you could have a shot at a medal. I really want to see you do well, and I believe you can. We've got less than two weeks to go till Regionals now, so whatever you've been doing, *keep doing it*."

Tara and Lindsay looked at each other. Tara knew that the afternoon practising at Lindsay's house, where they'd been able to relax, had made all the difference. But she couldn't do that again today – she'd already made plans with Kate and Emily.

"Do you want to come back to mine and get in a bit more practice?" asked Lindsay when they were in the changing room.

"I can't," said Tara. "I'm going to Emily's."

"Oh," replied Lindsay, surprised. They both knew it wasn't like Tara to refuse extra practice, especially after what Clare had just said. "That's fine," she said with a smile, after a second. "I have last-minute homework to do anyway."

When they came out of the gym, it was raining. Tara held her bag over her head and ran to the car, where Mum was waiting to take her to Emily's house. She had changed out of her leotard into jeans and a jumper. She'd forgotten to bring a hairbrush though, so she pulled her hair out of its ponytail and shook her head, combing through the blonde strands as well as she could with her fingers.

"Your hair's always so scruffy," sighed Mum. "You're going to have trouble getting it neat enough for the competition."

Tara just shrugged, then looked out of the window. She had way more to worry about for the competition than what her hair looked like. She flicked that thought away as she shook her hair again.

Emily's family owned a bakery and they lived above it. Mum pulled the car up by the row of shops and Tara opened the door immediately.

"Thanks! Bye!" she yelped, leaping out onto the pavement and making a dash for the bakery.

"Hi, Tara," said Mr. Walter, Emily's dad, who was standing behind the counter in the shop. "Go on upstairs, Kate's already here."

"Great, thanks," said Tara and she went

through the door at the back of the shop, past the kitchen and up the stairs to the Walters' flat. She could hear music coming from Emily's room and smiled to herself, imagining Kate singing and dancing along.

"Tara!" Emily smiled and jumped up off the bed when she came in.

"You're just in time," announced Kate, standing up on Emily's bed.

"For what?" Tara asked with a questioning smile at Emily.

"For me to paint your nails with my new nail varnish!" Kate replied, waving the tiny brush in the air with one hand, and holding the little glittery bottle up with the other.

"Is that the one you bought when we were shopping on Friday?" Tara asked. She sat down and untied her shoelaces, tugging off her Converse and shoving them in a corner.

"Yes," said Kate. "Now come here and I'll make your hands sparkle like mine and Em's."

"You went shopping without me?" asked Emily.

"For secret birthday things," Tara said, grinning. Kate giggled, taking one of Tara's hands.

"That's alright then," said Emily. "Go on as many secret birthday shopping trips as you want."

Emily and Kate started chatting about school. Tara half-listened to them for a while…but the trouble was that now she was here, she couldn't get rid of the niggling thought that she should be working on the routine. She tried to push it away. She was here with her best friends, and this was where she *wanted* to be…so why did she feel so guilty? But deep down she knew why: Clare expected her to do everything she could to win at Regionals. Tara looked at the glitter on her fingernails. This wasn't doing *everything*.

"So, about my birthday," said Emily suddenly. "Do you want to go to the cinema on Friday after school? I'm going to ask some other people from our year too. And you two could stay over afterwards."

"Yeah!" said Kate. "I thought you were never going to decide what to do for your party."

Tara stared down at her hands in silence. She had gym after school on Fridays and she'd secretly been hoping Emily would have a birthday party on the Saturday instead. It was one thing to choose her friends over extra practice at Lindsay's house. It was something completely different to decide not to go to Silverdale. Since Clare had told them about Regionals, none of the competing gymnasts had missed a single session. If it had been any other time of year... but with the competition only two weeks away, she didn't think she really had a choice.

"I don't think I can," she said quietly. "I'm so sorry, Em. I can't miss training. Not this close to the competition."

"That's okay," Emily said quickly, before Kate could start an argument. "I thought maybe... well, never mind. Maybe you can just come and sleep over?"

"Yeah, maybe," said Tara, thinking of the training session she would have on Saturday morning. Could she possibly make it through two hours of gymnastics after a sleepover?

Kate stared at Tara. She opened her mouth to say something, but then looked at Emily, who was obviously trying not to look hurt, and stopped. "Let's watch a film," suggested Kate.

Tara and Emily both sighed with relief, glad for a chance to pretend nothing was wrong. But Tara couldn't keep her mind on the story in the film. She kept replaying the birthday conversation in her mind, silently cringing at the look on Emily's face when she'd said she couldn't come.

This time, when Mum came to pick her up, it was Emily that she hugged fiercely. She wasn't sure that she'd made the right decision. But the party clashed with training at Silverdale – what else could she do? It was so hard though. She'd felt guilty about not doing extra practice, but that was nothing compared to this.

Friendships and Backflips

In bed that night she told herself that she *had* to choose gymnastics, even over Emily's birthday. But when she pulled the covers up over her head, she knew it wasn't true.

Chapter Twelve

"**I** can't believe you're not going to Emily's birthday," said Kate, as soon as Tara answered her phone the next evening. Tara hadn't seen her best friends at all during their first day back at school, except in maths. They'd disappeared at break time and lunch, and the "no mobiles" rule had made it impossible to find them. What made it even worse was that she'd told Lindsay she wanted to have lunch with her friends, so she didn't even see her gym partner. For the first time since starting secondary school, she'd felt completely alone.

"I can't. I wish I could." Tara curled her feet up underneath her on the sofa.

"You could if you wanted to. Em's too nice to say anything, but she's really upset."

"I have gym after school on Friday," Tara replied. "You know that."

"So? It wouldn't matter if you missed it once. You just don't want to."

"I *do*," Tara began, but it was too late. Instead of Kate's voice there was only silence. Tara could almost see her friend jabbing her finger on the *end call* button in a huff.

She was quiet during dinner that night feeling hurt by the way Kate had spoken to her.

"Mum," she said at last. "Do you think it would matter if I missed gym on Friday and went to Emily's birthday instead?"

"I'm sure missing one training session won't

hurt," replied Mum thoughtfully. "What do you want to do?"

"I want to do both, but I can't."

"Well, which one is more important?" asked Dad.

Tara thought about it while she twirled some spaghetti around her fork. "The gym competition is really, really important and I need to train for it every minute I can," she said. She paused and bit her lip. "But I think if Emily didn't come to *my* birthday, it would feel horrible."

Mum nodded and smiled at her.

"I think you should go to Emily's," said Anna, looking up from the mess of spaghetti she'd made on her plate. "Birthdays are much more fun than boring gymnastics."

Tara wished it was that simple.

Monday turned into Tuesday, and that became Wednesday. By Wednesday afternoon, Tara still hadn't decided what to do. She was almost sure she was going to skip Friday's training session, but she hadn't got up the courage to ask Clare yet, and she hadn't told Emily. She wanted to go to the cinema with the others, to have fun and sing "Happy Birthday" to her best friend, but something was still holding her back. She wanted to be a good gymnast, and great gymnasts took their training seriously. Was there a way to have both things – to be a good friend to Emily and to be a serious gymnast too?

At the end of training on Wednesday, Tara hung back and waited until Clare had finished talking to Jack.

"What's up, Tara?" the coach asked with a smile. It had been a great training session and she was in a good mood. That made Tara feel a little less nervous.

"I was wondering…" She swallowed and took a deep breath. "Would it be okay if I miss training on Friday?" The words rushed out and she looked hopefully up at her coach.

"Why?" Clare asked.

"It's...um, it's my best friend's birthday," Tara said hesitantly. She thought that probably sounded really lame to Clare. She wished she could have thought of a way to say it that made it sound as important as it really was.

Clare paused, considering it. "You've been working harder than anyone," she said finally. "I don't think missing one session will ruin that. You deserve a break. Just make sure you're not too tired to train hard on Saturday!"

"Thanks, Clare!" Tara grinned. She rose up on tiptoe in her excitement and gave her coach a quick hug. "I *promise* I'll make up for it by being extra brilliant on Saturday!"

The next morning, Tara's maths class were working on questions from their textbooks. She tore a page from the back of her exercise book and wrote a note to Emily.

Sorry I was stupid and said no to your birthday. Can I still come?
xxx

She folded the paper, wrote Emily's name on the front, and asked the girl sitting behind her to pass it back towards her friends in the opposite corner of the room. She turned and watched the note travel from hand to hand.

Emily read it. She looked up with a big smile and nodded enthusiastically. Then she scrunched the note up in her fist before Mr. Spencer could see it. Tara grinned back and settled down to work. She knew she'd made the right choice.

The next day was Friday, and Emily's twelfth birthday. A few people gave her birthday cards in the morning, and Tara and Kate both gave her presents. Mum had taken Tara shopping after school on Thursday so that she could buy something. Emily opened Kate's first – a pair of pink and silver dangly earrings. Emily had had her ears pierced last month and she was dying to start wearing pretty earrings instead of plain silver studs.

"Thanks, Kate. I'll wear them this evening!" she said, and then spun around to face Tara. "You're still coming, aren't you?" Worry crossed her face until Tara nodded.

"Of course!" She was going to say sorry again for being a bad friend at first, but Emily threw her arms around her before she could speak. The present from Tara, still wrapped in pale blue tissue paper, was forgotten in her hand. Tara laughed. "Aren't you going to open your present?" she asked. Emily jumped back and began carefully opening the paper.

"Tear it!" groaned Kate. "I want to see what it is." Emily smiled and slowly peeled back the paper. Inside was a photo frame with silvery flowers around the edges. Behind the glass was a photo of Emily, Kate and Tara. Tara's dad had taken it in Kate's garden in the summer, when the three of them had performed a dance show for their parents. Their hair blew about their faces, blonde tangling with dark and dark with light brown. They had their arms draped around each other's shoulders and were laughing at a joke none of them could remember any more.

"Thank you," Emily said softly. "I love it."

After school, the three girls and a few of their other friends went back to Emily's house, where they ate pizza and then sang "Happy Birthday" before Emily blew out twelve candles on a beautiful cake. Mrs. Walter had made the cake herself. It was covered with white icing, and there were lilac coloured flowers in a circle around the top. In the middle, *Happy Birthday, Emily* was written in lilac icing. After they'd eaten a delicious slice each, Mrs. Walter took them all to the cinema. She bought their tickets and told them what time to meet her afterwards, and then they went into the film by themselves.

They giggled and whispered through the funny parts, and Kate pretended to cry when the film was supposed to be sad. Later, they sang pop songs all the way back to Emily's house. They gossiped about school and listened to music for a while, and soon it was time for the other girls to go home.

Kate, Tara and Emily changed into pyjamas and laid the big cushions from the sofa on the floor of Emily's room, with sleeping bags and blankets. They all sat on Emily's bed, eating sweets and trying to keep their laughter quiet so that they didn't wake Emily's younger brothers. They talked until the early hours of the morning about everything they had missed chatting about while Tara was at gym. Tara noticed that Emily and Kate had a lot more to talk about than she did. Once she'd told them a bit about gymnastics, there wasn't much else to say. Eventually, Tara and Kate moved to their sleeping bags on the floor, their eyes began to close, and after a while Tara heard Kate's breathing turn into quiet snoring.

"Tara?" Emily whispered, after it had been silent for a while.

"Yes?"

"I'm really glad you came." Tara lay on her back, staring up at the ceiling of Emily's bedroom where there were a few glow-in-the-dark stars. "I know you had to miss gym," continued Emily, still whispering so she didn't wake Kate. "And I understand why you didn't want to. So thanks. It just wouldn't have felt like my birthday without you."

"That's okay," Tara murmured. She heard Emily turn over in her bed to go to sleep. But Tara's eyes were still wide open. "Em?" she whispered.

"Yeah?"

"I'm really glad I came, too."

Even though she couldn't see her friend in the dark, Tara knew that Emily was smiling just as much as she was. She turned on her side and closed her eyes. Mum was picking her up early the next morning to go to Silverdale, and she knew she'd be exhausted. But it was absolutely, completely worth it.

Chapter Thirteen

The last week before Regionals passed quickly. Lindsay and Tara focused on getting everything as precise and beautiful as possible, but they had fun too. Working hard every minute of every day could make gymnastics feel like a chore, and that wasn't what they wanted. They only had one lunchtime practice, and Emily and Kate came to watch. They were amazed by what their friend could do.

"Can we come to the competition?" begged Kate.

"Of course!" Tara smiled. "I've wanted to ask you for ages, but I thought you hated gymnastics."

"No way," said Kate. "We just got annoyed that it was taking over your life."

"We'd love to come," Emily added. "You're our best friend and we want to cheer you on."

"And go wild when you win the gold medal," Kate said, grinning.

Tara laughed. She felt nervous whenever anyone mentioned winning. She and Lindsay had trained so hard, but what if it still wasn't enough?

At the end of lunchtime, Kate and Emily talked excitedly about the competition and the balances Tara and Lindsay could do all the way back to their form rooms. Tara was thrilled that they were coming to watch her compete, but every extra pair of eyes on her was an extra bit of pressure. Her friends, her parents, her sister…they really wanted to see her win, but they didn't know how high the standard would be. Would she let them all down? And what about Clare? She had taken a risk letting Tara and Lindsay compete at Regionals, and Tara was desperate to make her coach proud.

The competition was on a Saturday in the middle of November. Tara and the rest of the Silverdale squad had to be at the gym at eight o'clock in the morning for one last practice. Jittering in the cold changing room, they were all strung up on butterflies and hopeful excitement. On the familiar blue floor, they performed their routines better than they ever had before, and they all hoped that they could do just as well that afternoon.

The competition was being held at Central Gym Club, which was in a nearby town and was the biggest club in the area. When they arrived, Tara looked around with wide eyes and gaping mouth. It was *huge*. There were three gyms, all with big open spaces and lots of equipment. Most of the others had been in club competitions there before, so they knew their way around. As Jasmine led the way to the changing rooms, Tara peeked through the door of the second gym they passed. She guessed that this gym wasn't being used for the competition; there were small groups of gymnasts working on each piece of apparatus and it looked like just another training day. It wasn't as noisy as Silverdale usually was on Saturdays. It might have been all the extra space to move in, but Tara thought it seemed somehow colder, too.

She hurried after Jasmine and the others. It wasn't hard to tell where the changing room was – it was the noisiest room in the whole building! When Sophie pushed the door open, they stepped into a bright room full of colour and chatter. They found a space and changed quickly into their leotards. Tara smiled when she put hers on – she loved it more than any other item of clothing she'd ever owned. Then she stood still while Jasmine pulled her hair back into a neat bun, which was encircled by a dark blue scrunchie. She was so busy taking everything in that she hardly even noticed how hard Jasmine was pulling.

When she emerged from the white cloud of hairspray, she caught sight of herself in the mirror. She looked like a gymnast – and suddenly she felt the full excitement of competing. She was nervous, but she couldn't wait to get out there and perform her routine. This was what she'd been waiting for ever since she'd first begun to practise wobbly handstands in the garden.

"Put your tracksuit on, you need to keep warm," Sam told her, for once speaking to Tara the same way she would talk to any of the more experienced gymnasts. *The importance of the competition must be getting to her,* Tara thought. She obediently covered up the beloved leotard with her new Silverdale tracksuit. There were gymnasts everywhere, in leotards and tracksuits of every colour and pattern imaginable. Everyone was chattering loudly; it sounded like the lunch hall at school.

"Ready, everyone?" demanded Sam. "Let's go out then, it's chaos in here. I told the boys to meet us in the corridor." They followed her out of the changing room, where the boys were waiting, and into the gym. It was already starting to fill up with people, even though there was still an hour until the competition started.

Clare gathered them together and led them into the warm-up room, which was an extra gym usually used for working on floor routines. There was no other equipment, just a sprung floor and a wall of mirrors. Other teams were also trickling through and beginning to warm up. Tara looked at them all, trying to size up the competition.

"Tara, are you listening?" demanded Clare. "Ignore everyone else. Focus on your routine. Only the routine." She talked them through some reminders and picked up on a few things she'd noticed in their morning practice. "Sophie, you *must* make sure you point your toes, and Tara, keep your eyes up no matter how nervous you are!"

Friendships and Backflips

They warmed up in a small group, facing each other so that they wouldn't be distracted by the gymnasts all around them practising balances. In no time at all, Clare stopped them and told them it was competition time. Everyone was starting to go back into the main gym, and they tacked onto the end of the line leaving the warm-up room. They found their place on the benches reserved for the gymnasts, which ran all the way along two of the walls. Tara saw her parents and Anna in the crowd of spectators and waved. Then she saw Emily and Kate sitting next to them and waved even harder, as they waved excitedly back at her. Knowing that they were here to see her perform and cheer her on made the whole competition even more special.

A man with a microphone walked into the middle of the floor.

"Welcome to the Regional Acrobatic Gymnastics Competition!" he announced. "I'd like to invite the gymnasts to present themselves, and then we'll get going." Tara and the others got up and joined the long, colourful line walking round the floor. She was so excited that it was hard not to laugh. She'd seen Olympic gymnasts march round the gym at the beginning of competitions, and now she was doing it herself!

The audience clapped and cheered while the competitors walked around the blue square where all the drama of the afternoon was about to happen. Then the gymnasts sat back down on the benches and settled themselves to watch their rivals. There were two floor areas. Luckily the girls' pairs were competing on the same floor as the boys' groups, while the boys' pairs, mixed pairs and girls' trios were on the other floor – Tara thought Clare must be relieved that all the Silverdale gymnasts would be in the same place.

Sam and Jasmine's competition was first. They were the third pair to compete, and they performed their routine brilliantly. Despite all the nasty comments Sam had made, Tara had to admit that the older gymnast was really, really good. Tara watched the other Level 4 pairs, dreaming of the day that she'd be able to do the things they did. There were flicks and somersaults, and lots of the tops did handstands on their partners' hands. Tara imagined doing that on Lindsay's hands and a shiver ran down her spine. A few months ago she'd have laughed and thought it was impossible, but now…well, who knew?

No one was surprised when Jasmine and Sam scored the highest, winning the first gold medal for Silverdale.

"You're so lucky, going near the beginning," grumbled Jack, when they joined the others again. "Now you can enjoy the rest of the competition."

The next round was Level 4 boys, but there were no Silverdale gymnasts competing in that category. Then it was Level 3 girls. Tara could see Megan and Sophie on the other side of the floor, waiting for their turn. Megan was lightly bouncing up and down on the balls of her feet and Sophie was swinging her arms around vigorously. Neither of them could keep still. Just watching them made Tara feel nervous.

Some of the other pairs in Megan and Sophie's level were very good, but lots of them were messy and made mistakes. Some had graceful classical music, others performed to fun, bouncy tunes, and a few matched their gymnastics to spiky electronic sounds that made Tara think of spaceships and robots. Watching them, Tara noticed all the things that Clare would have criticized; some were not quite in time with each other, some didn't point their toes or stretch their arms enough. One girl looked down at the floor for the whole routine, and another didn't finish any of her balances properly. She looked as if she was just doing a rough practice! Tara tucked all these things away in her mind so that she wouldn't make the same mistakes.

Megan and Sophie sailed through their routine with no problems. They even had the crowd clapping along to their rhythmic music while they bounced in and out of powerful handsprings and backflips. Clare had explained to Tara that their routines would be scored out of thirty – ten marks for the difficulty of the routine, ten marks for how well they performed the gymnastics skills, and ten marks for performance. Tara bet that Megan and Sophie had got themselves lots of points for being so wonderful to watch. There was a burst of loud applause when they performed their final balance; Sophie was in a bridge position on the floor, and Megan held a steady handstand on Sophie's stomach. Tara had seen it go wrong lots of times in the gym, but when it mattered Megan and Sophie held the balance as if it was the simplest thing in the world. The audience loved them, and they walked off the floor to the sound of whooping and clapping. Tara was pleased for them, and thrilled to see another gold medal go to Silverdale, but she couldn't help being a little bit envious. They made it seem so easy.

The four boys from Silverdale were in the next round, but Tara and Lindsay didn't get to see them perform. Their competition was afterwards, so they were lost in their own little world in the warm-up gym. Even if they had been allowed to watch, Tara was sure she'd never be able to concentrate on anything but the thought of her own routine at that moment. There was hardly any time left until she had to go out and prove to Sam and Clare and everyone else that she deserved to be here, wearing the Silverdale competition leotard…to prove that she deserved to be in Clare's squad.

When they walked back into the gym, Tara glanced quickly at the Silverdale bench. The boys didn't look very excited, and Jasmine's face was full of sympathy. They were the first Silverdale gymnasts not to win gold, Tara guessed. Would she and Lindsay be the second? She started to feel sick.

They were competing near the end of the

round, so they had to watch most of the other Level 2 pairs first. There was one light, bouncy routine that she really enjoyed, and another which was full of graceful steps to gorgeous flowing music. They were serious competition. The graceful routine finished, and Tara and Lindsay exchanged nervous grins. They were next. They rubbed chalk on their hands and feet to stop themselves slipping in balances, just as the score for the pair before them went up: 28.3. It was the highest score so far.

Chapter Fourteen

Tara's heart was beating faster than their jazzy music. She and Lindsay walked out onto the floor, and stepped forward with their arms stretched up to present themselves to the judges. Then they took up their starting positions and the familiar music began. It sounded much louder in the big gym, with everyone watching. They jumped and turned their way through Clare's lovely routine, their handsprings and split leaps perfectly in time with the upbeat, cheerful music. Tara smiled and kept her chin up, directing her expressive arm movements out towards the audience. Her walkovers felt smooth and effortless. The springy floor helped her to bounce out of a round-off into a full turn jump, spinning through the air and landing neatly with her feet together, facing Lindsay.

In a second Tara found herself at Lindsay's side, preparing for their toughest challenge. Her palms were sweating but she took Lindsay's hands and pulled herself up to stand on her shoulders, perfectly in time with the music. She made sure she was balancing securely, then she lifted one foot...held onto it...and stretched her leg up into the Y-balance. It felt wonderful!

She held her head high with a joyful smile and drank in the applause that burst from the audience. Then she came down neatly, and they flew through another section full of dance and gymnastics skills, including one-handed cartwheels and walkovers into the splits. When Lindsay held Tara above her head in front angel, Tara knew the routine was nearly finished. She raised her head. Her arms were held beautifully out to the sides and her toes were pointed. She felt like she was flying. In only a few seconds, they'd have got through the whole routine without any mistakes, but Tara didn't want it to end.

They held their final poses for a second, breathless but smiling, and then walked neatly off the floor, to the sound of loud applause. Tara couldn't make out Emily and Kate's voices, but she knew that they'd be cheering louder than anyone. As soon as Tara and Lindsay's feet left the springy floor, they became a huddle of blue velvet hugs and laughter.

"We held it!" Tara and Lindsay squealed to each other at exactly the same time.

"Good job, you two," Sam said, nodding.

"I was sure I couldn't hold on in counterbalance," gabbled Tara. "My feet were so slippy!

Good thing you were gripping me so tightly!"

Sophie laughed. "We felt like that too! We'll all need to use more chalk when we go to Nationals."

Tara and Lindsay stopped talking and looked at Sophie. Nationals. Had their routine been good enough to get them there? They sat down as the judges finished making notes. Clare gave them a thumbs up and Tara grinned.

"You two did a really good routine," Clare said. Tara was desperate to know if they had a chance of winning, but her coach's face gave nothing away.

The lead judge shuffled around some scorecards. Tara gripped Lindsay's hand on one side and Jasmine's on the other. The judge finally held up their score. 28.5   they were in first place, with only two pairs to go!

Tara could hardly bear to watch the last routines. All she cared about were the black and white cards that came at the end. One pair were good but slightly messy, and the others had played it safe and only performed very easy balances and gymnastic movements.

At last the final scores were in, and cheers went up from the Silverdale bench: Tara and Lindsay were the winners. They were Regional Champions! Tara kept thinking those words, over and over again, unable to believe it was true. She was still full of the feeling she'd had on the floor, excitement and nervousness all mixed up into one brilliant kind of energy.

After that, everything passed in an ecstatic blur. There were hugs all round, all over again. All six of the Silverdale girls had got through to the Nationals. The boys were disappointed not to be going too, but they were happy for the girls and if they were jealous, they didn't let it show.

Tara couldn't wait to compete again – the Nationals would be even bigger, even better! She twisted round on the bench and tried to catch Kate and Emily's eyes. Anna waved madly with a huge smile. Kate and Emily were so excited they looked like they might fall out of their seats. Having her best friends there as a part of this moment made winning feel even more perfect.

The medal-winning gymnasts from all levels were announced and when Tara heard her name called along with Lindsay's, her stomach did backflips all over again. She could hardly believe this was really happening. They took their places on the floor to the sound of applause and medals were hung around their necks. Tara still felt as if she was flying – even higher than when she was held high above Lindsay's head.

"We did it!" whispered Lindsay. "We *won*."

Tara looked down at her medal shining against her navy blue leotard. She was a real gymnast at a real competition, and now she'd even won a gold medal. It was her favourite daydream come true! She knew that she was going to relive this moment again and again. But then she smiled up at her family and at Kate and Emily and she realized that their cheering and clapping meant more to her than any medal ever could. She was lucky enough to have her friends, her family *and* gym. She looked at Lindsay and the others, with their matching gold medals, and thought there was only one way she could possibly be any happier. And that was a whole competition away. A National competition.

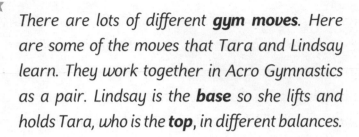

There are lots of different **gym moves**. Here are some of the moves that Tara and Lindsay learn. They work together in Acro Gymnastics as a pair. Lindsay is the **base** so she lifts and holds Tara, who is the **top**, in different balances.

Backflip: a move where Tara swings her arms back and pushes off with her feet. She lands on her hands with her body arched then flips her legs up and over her head, then she pushes off with her hands to land back on both feet.

Backward walkover: Tara bends over backwards from a standing position with one leg raised until her hands reach the floor and her body forms an arch. Her legs then kick over, passing through the splits, to land standing up again.

Balance: where Tara holds a fixed pose with Lindsay.

Counter-balance: Lindsay stands with her knees bent and feet apart. Tara stands on Lindsay's thighs, facing her. They grip each other's wrists, both then lean back until their arms are straight.

Front somersault: Tara turns head over heels in the air in a tucked shape to land back on her feet.

Handspring: a move where Tara lunges into a handstand, then flips over onto her feet.

Round-off: a fast cartwheel which Tara springs out of and lands on two feet.

Standing front angel: Lindsay stands up straight and holds Tara above her head. Tara balances horizontally in a T shape with Lindsay's hands on her hips.

Standing on shoulders balance: *Tara stands with one foot on each of Lindsay's shoulders while Lindsay holds onto her calves. They can do this with Lindsay kneeling down, kneeling up with one foot on the floor, or standing.*

Straddle: *in this position Tara sits on the floor with her legs out wide making a right angle.*

Straddle lever balance: *Tara balances on her hands with her legs held in the straddle position.*

Y-balance: *standing on one leg, Tara holds her other foot with her hand and stretches her leg out to the side, so that her body forms a Y shape.*

Tara's Gym Star dreams
continue in these dazzling titles:

Jane Lawes

Gym Stars

Summertime and
Somersaults

Foreword by
BETH TWEDDLE
OLYMPIC
Medal Winner

ISBN: 9781474922937

Jane Lawes

Gym Stars

Handsprings and
Homework

Foreword by
BETH TWEDDLE
OLYMPIC
Medal Winner

ISBN: 9781474922951

Also by Jane Lawes:

Ballet Stars

Follow Tash's adventures at Aurora House,
the boarding ballet school where dancing
dreams come true!

ISBN: 9781409583530

ISBN: 9781409583547

ISBN: 9781409583554

Usborne Quicklinks

For links to websites where you can watch video clips of gymnastics routines and find out more about balances and basic skills and gymnastics organizations, go to the Usborne Quicklinks website at www.usborne.com/quicklinks and enter the keywords "gym stars".

Please read the internet safety guidelines displayed at the Usborne Quicklinks website.

For more dazzling reads head to
www.usborne.com/fiction